Rodney's Inside Story

Lynne Barasch

Orchard Books · New York

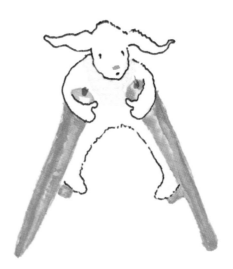

Thank you, Brooke Goffstein, Sidney Offit, and Ellen Schwartz,
for your help, so generously given. And, always, Ken.

Orchard Books, 95 Madison Avenue, New York, NY 10016

Manufactured in the United States of America
Printed by Barton Press, Inc. Bound by Horowitz/Rae.
Book design by Mina Greenstein
The text of this book is set in ITC Baskerville and Helvetica.
The illustrations are watercolor with pen-and-ink.

10 9 8 7 6 5 4 3 2 1

Library of Congress Cataloging-in-Publication Data
Barasch, Lynne. Rodney's inside story / by Lynne Barasch.   p.   cm.
Summary: Mommy tells a story about Rodney Rabbit, who lives inside a cabbage and
has lots of vegetables to play with.
ISBN 0-531-05993-6.   ISBN 0-531-08593-7 (lib. bdg.)
[1. Rabbits—Fiction.   2. Vegetables—Fiction.]   I. Title.
PZ7.B22965Ro   1992   [E]—dc20   91-24405

For all of you and because of you—
Wendy, Jill, Nina, Cassie, and Dinah

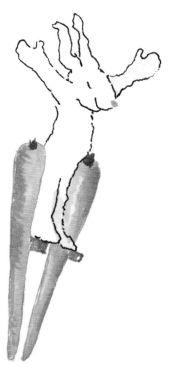

"Now that you're all tucked in for your nap, Baby Gray, here is the story of Rodney Rabbit," says Mommy.

"Rodney Rabbit lives in a cabbage.

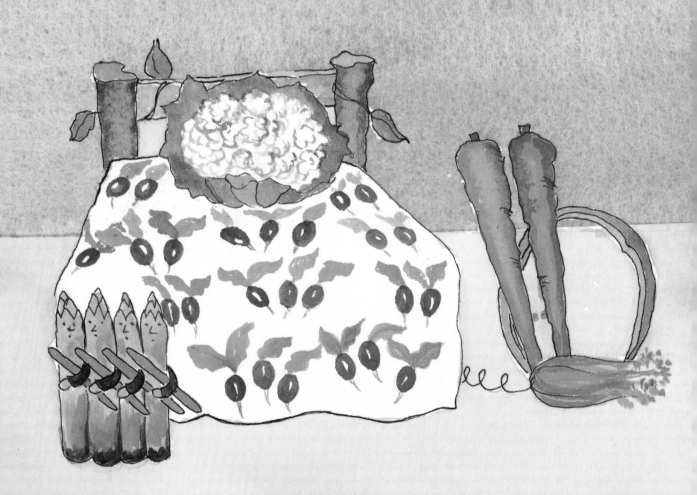

"This is his room.

"In it, he has tomatoes to juggle,

a green pepper hula hoop to spin,

an onion skin to make a paper airplane,

carrot stilts to stand on,

asparagus soldiers that shoot lentils
from string bean guns,

a celery phone to call on,

a radish doll to hug,

and an eggplant desk to sit behind.

"Rodney often reads a book about a
little gray rabbit who looks just like
you, Baby Gray. This is the story
Rodney reads.

Baby Gray lives with his family

in a hollow under a tree.

The Grays' favorite pastime is eating.

They take tomatoes and peppers and onions and carrots,

asparagus and string beans and celery and radishes to a picnic.

They eat and eat and eat and eat and eat and eat

and eat and eat,

till no one can eat another bite.

"The story makes Rodney hungry,

so he takes some beet cookies from
his artichoke cookie jar and eats
them.

"Now Rodney is ready for his nap. He puts his head on his cauliflower pillow and goes to sleep."

So does Baby Gray.